Rig

CW01497976

Published |

This is for anyone who actually makes it through to the end of the book and does not hate me.

Summary

After receiving news of his father's untimely death Tyler Rydek sets out on a journey back to his childhood home, he learns quickly that he wasn't the only one keeping secrets in that house.

Warning

I'm told this book should have an 'extreme' warning.

Because these things are always in my head and on my mind, I don't always consider them to be over- the- top. To some it may be run- of- the mill and to others it may be too much.

If you feel like you may have issues reading 'extreme' stories please do not bother with this one, you may be offended.

I do not condone any of this shit in real life, please remember this is a work of fiction and as always do not try this at home.

There are graphic scenes and disgusting things within these pages… you have been warned.

Chapter One

"Hello, am I speaking with Tyler Rydek?"

The unknown number that I answered thinking it was Cammie calling from a friend's phone asks. I should not be in charge of my devices after a night of binge drinking. I can barely think right now.

"Yea," I say, rolling over onto my side to look at the alarm clock. Seven fucking thirty. Who the fuck calls someone at 7:30am?

I stumble into the bathroom, bumping into the wall as I pass, unsteady on my still drunken feet, not fully listening to the man's voice. He's going on about something I can't hear over the stream of alcohol pushing its way out of my mornings semi-hardened cock.

"What's this about?" I ask after climbing back into bed, pulling the covers over my naked body up to my chin. I must have left a window open last night. The chill in here is too much. I think about going to close it but I can't climb back out of the covers to do so right now.

"Mr. Rydek, I'm your father's attorney. I'm sorry to be the one to tell you this… but he has passed. The hospital called last night, he had been mugged– stabbed multiple times by the assailant. He didn't recover. There was too much damage to his organs. They thought he would be alright after surgery, but he passed while he was sleeping."

I can't wrap my head around this. My father was 45 years old, still young and full of life. "Did they catch the guy?" I ask.

"No, no witnesses were at the scene when he was found. A woman came across him lying there in the alley. She told police he was the only one there when she arrived."

"Wow." I don't know what else to say. It hasn't hit me yet, the words he's saying should be enough to effect me, to bring the tears. He was my best friend, a great father, the man I idolized growing up. My hero. But, they don't come, I don't cry, instead I ask him why he is the one calling me.

"He gave me strict instructions upon making his Will that I be the one to call if he were to meet his fate. I'm simply following his request."

"Oh, so what now?" I ask, not sure I even want to know. My eyes are getting heavy with sleep.

"I'll ask that you come to my office, he has some things he'd like me to give you personally. Then we can go over his last Will and Testament."

"Where's my mother?" I haven't talked to her in years, she is the reason I had to get out of that fucking town. She's a lot to handle. And that is the fucking understatement of a lifetime.

"Mr. Rydek, I have no idea of your mother's whereabouts. I'm your father's attorney. I had no dealings with her."

"Ok. So, when should we do this?"

"I'd like it to be as soon as possible, he's told me there are time sensitive things for you."

"Well, I can't be there sooner than tomorrow night. It's a long drive for me; I'm no longer in town."

"That should be fine; I'll have everything ready for your arrival."

"I need an address." I look around the room, I don't even think I own a pen to take it down, but it's a small town, I should have been able to retain enough to find it.

"Absolutely, I'm at the old textile loft on First Street. Are you familiar with the building?"

Oh, fuck, that old loft was the hang out for all the stoners; of course I know the place. "Yea, I know where you're at. I'll be there tomorrow night. Thanks for the call."

"I'll see you then, sir. I'm so sorry for your loss; your father was truly a great man– a friend of mine for years."

"Thanks, I'm sorry you lost him, too, then." I push end on my cell before he can say anything else, pulling the comforter over my face to warm my nose I pass out in seconds.

Chapter Two

The morning– or afternoon rather, comes quicker than I am ready for it. The sun coming from the large bay window is beating down on my face.

I pick up my phone and check for a missed call from Cammie. Nothing. She is so good at avoiding me. I roll my eyes at her antics, I don't know why I even want a fucking girlfriend, they are definitely more trouble than they're worth. The occasional blowjob or fuck is not worth the hassle of all the emotional bullshit I have had to tolerate from them– her in particular. Say or do the wrong thing and this girl will fight with you for a week and ignore you for a second one.

It's becoming too much for me. Still, she does have the best ass and tits I've ever seen– when she actually lets me have access to them, that is. The girl is also very much a prude, little miss catholic school girl– and the kind that doesn't go wild and fuck anyone and everything. She's the boring kind that wants you to marry her and shit. That's not for me, but I tell her whatever she wants to hear to let me inside. She gave me her virginity after some major manipulation on my part to get her to do it. I'm not giving up on that tight hole before I'm done with it.

I climb my hung- over ass out of bed, remembering the call from earlier, I think of all the things I need to do to be ready to head out soon. It's going to be a long night of driving, nearly a thousand miles. I could not have gotten far enough away when I left.

I relieve myself then head into the kitchen for coffee, passing the front door that is standing wide open– the source of the cold last night. Not the first time I've neglected to close it. The damn thing swings wide open if I don't slam it.

I do now, the thunderous sound shaking the walls.

The smell of coffee brewing is finally doing something to rouse my mind– waking me. My mouth is salivating for the dark drink. I take a too- big swallow of it after it's done. Burning my mouth, but not caring, I go for a second one, topping my cup off before heading back to my room to get packed and ready for the trip.

I pull on a pair of jeans after loading a few other pairs into my bag, throwing some tees on top of the stack and then call Cammie's phone. Voicemail. I leave her a message explaining why I'll be gone for the next few days and that I need to talk to her and then slip the phone into my back pocket. I pull on a t-shirt and my favorite hoodie and take the bag to my car.

I look around the house before leaving, making a quick checklist of things I may have overlooked. I can't think of anything more I'll need while I'm there so I fill a travel mug with the remainder of the coffee and lock up the house.

Chapter Three

I've always hated this drive. After leaving my parent's house and coming here for college, I've made the trek a few times. Before I didn't, choosing one day not to go back.

When college was over, I got a job, got a house, got a life and didn't want this fucking town to be a part of it anymore. So, it wasn't.

I've been on the road for almost three hours, making my way through my favorite playlist when I see a girl on the side of the road– telltale hitch hiker thumb up. I don't give it much thought, I just pull over to the side of the road when I reach her. She is blonde and tall, short skirt and a top that shows off her tits. Her face is nice, but not beautiful– I notice when she sticks her head in the window I opened for her.

"I'm going about a hundred miles west, think you could help me out?" she sounds sweet, but the eyes she's giving me tells me she may be a little naughty.

"I can do that." I tell her, hitting the button to unlock the door for her.

"Thank you." She throws her bag into the back seat. "What's your name?" she asks after settling into the seat next to me.

"Tyler." I say, looking a little too long at her thighs, exposed after her skirt gets hiked up from sitting.

She notices, opening them slightly more– possibly subconsciously. I've always had a way with the ladies. My all- American boy good looks have made it easy for me to get what and whom I want. I run my hand through my shaggy blond hair and look her in the eye; my eyebrow goes up in a way that tells her I know that she wants me. The way she bites her bottom lip lets me know I was right.

"I'm April."

Before pulling away I ask her, "So, April, you got gas money?" I don't really want it, I want her to offer something else in return.

"I don't have any money."

Good. "What else could you repay this kind favor with?" My cock is growing in my pants just thinking about the possibilities.

"Umm, what do you want?" she asks, squirming a little in her seat, showing me she knows what it might be.

I reach my hand over to her face, sliding my thumb in between her lips and she fucking lets me.

Slut.

"How about you put this to work?"

Her tongue tastes my thumb, sending a shock to my dick. "I could do that," she says shyly. The shy shit must be all an act because she's far too eager to get her hands on my zipper.

The feel of her warm mouth on my excited cock makes me hiss. Her ass is high in the air, knees on her seat as she leans over the console in the center. I can see her cheeks peeking out of the skirt. I pull it up more, exposing her completely. Her little black thong is tucked nicely in between. I give one side a smack and she moans, humming around my cock. The girl is good at it, she is taking me deep– I can feel the back of her throat against the head.

I tuck my hand under her– between her legs. She spreads to accommodate it. I feel how wet she is instantly– her panties are soaked. I bypass them quickly and slip my fingers into the slit of her meaty pussy.

She moans again, growing hungrier for me. My finger finds her hole and I push inside of her without a care. Her juicy cunt is all too excited for me. The wet sounds coming from her hole as I pump my hand quickly mingle nicely with the sounds of her throat fucking me.

I wrap my fingers into her hair and hold her tightly in place, bucking my hips to reach past her tonsils. She gags but doesn't try and pull away. Her pussy accepts another of my fingers and she rocks against them.

I get lost in the feel of her throat, my thoughts go to Cammie– she would never let me do anything like this. Sure, she's ok with the occasional blowjob but I'd never get her to deep throat me. She is more a put your mouth around the head until I tell her it's good enough and to stop so we can "make love" and then spreading her shy legs in missionary position until I come– which often times takes too long, as she likes it slow and sweet.

This girl here can really take a cock. I might have to take advantage of this again before I let her out.

My hips buck faster, pushing deeply into her, her breathing is labored and the noises coming from her throat encourage me. The sound of her gagging as she takes my cock thrills me and I'm so fucking close to coming. "Are you going to let me come in your mouth?"

She nods, barely able to move.

"You want to taste me, don't you?"

Another nod.

"You gonna swallow it?"

She moans in reply.

"You're a hungry little slut, aren't you?"

"Mmhmm."

I pull my fingers out of her and the bitch fucking whines like a dog in heat. "Make yourself come for me. I want you coming with me so hurry the fuck up."

Her hand works her clit fast, I watch as her arm moves quickly, rubbing herself aggressively.

I tilt her head so I can see more of her face to watch how my cock looks inside her mouth. Her eyes are wet from choking and her mascara has made her look like a raccoon. She has her jaw wide but her lips wrapped tight. I move her head slowly up my shaft; her lips pop as I leave her mouth. Then I push my swelling cock back in, her throat accommodating me now that it has been accustomed to the girth.

She tries to keep her eyes on mine but I fuck her faster– crashing her face into me. It makes her come only seconds later, her mouth losing focus on me a little but it gives me my opportunity to really fuck it– with her mind on her own orgasm I pound her mouth harder than is polite, ravaging her throat.

I'm grunting hard at the effort and her choking- throat milks my coming- cock as she struggles to swallow the load down. Her head pops up as soon as I let it go, she coughs and tries to catch her breath. I see a dribble of my come on her chin– her lipstick- smeared lips adding to the beautiful picture, making her look thoroughly fucked.

I don't know if I've scared her, so I'm hesitant to say anything. I've not had the privilege to do something like that to anyone's mouth. I don't know what she's feeling right now. So, I take this moment to tuck my cock into my pants and wait patiently for any hint of her thoughts.

I know she's ok when she starts to giggle.

My neck snaps at the sound. I catch her eyes immediately and I'm struck by the huge smile on her face.

"Well, you really like head, don't you?" licking the last bit of my milky white dribble

I don't know what to say to her, so I put the car in gear and take us back on to the road, peeking occasionally at the advances she's making at cleaning the makeup from her face. No longer looking like a clown, she goes about reapplying it.

"There, good as new," she says suddenly, announcing her job is done.

I turn the radio down and take a look at her efforts. "Very good," is what I say. Back to the boring girl she was before I face- fucked her.

"I've never done anything like that before."

"Could've fooled me," I joke.

"I mean I've sucked a dick before, but never like that and never for a ride. I am not a hooker."

"Didn't think you were; although, you'd make a pretty good one if you ever change your mind." I look over to see how she has taken my joke.

She just smiles that shy smile from before. "Where are you going?" she asks.

"My father just died, I'm going back to check on my mom and talk about the Will and shit."

"I'm sorry," is all she says. I don't ask her any questions, we're just about to her drop off and I don't want her lingering.

"Anywhere in particular you want me to drop you?" The signs are announcing her destination now.

"There's a convenience store right after the exit… if you don't mind."

"That works," I say, looking at the fuel gage and realizing I should fill up while I'm there. My stomach growls to remind me that it's empty as well.

I pull up to a pump and she grabs her bag from the back, throwing the strap over her shoulder. "Thank you for the ride, Tyler," she says.

"Any time, doll," I respond back to her, giving her a wink.

She blushes before turning to go inside the store.

I put my debit card into the slot at the pump and watch as the numbers tick upward until they come to a stop once it's full. Then I pull the car into a spot and head inside to see if they have some sort of deli. They do not, I realize quickly. It's too small in here for much of anything. I grab a candy bar and a coffee to hold me over until I stop again and wave at April as I go.

She waves back, looking around self-consciously to see if any one notices.

Back on the road, I'm lost in the thoughts I was able to keep at bay with that girl next to me. I regret not taking her into the restroom and fucking her, but it's too late now to turn back, I'll just have to live with the 'what if'.

I laugh at the thought of her screams echoing in that small store. The old clerk would have lost his shit at the sounds that would be coming from her as I fucked her, her hot little pussy wet and dripping for me, pounding into her from behind.

I let out a frustrated breath. I don't want to work myself up any more than I have so I take my hand from my hardened cock and inhale deeply, pushing those thoughts away with the long and slow exhale.

I have not masturbated in years, too much time was being wasted on that when the real thing could happen effortlessly enough. I'm not going to start now, not for that girl.

I turn up the radio and let my mind get lost in the lyrics, singing along when I know them.

It gets dark quickly, considering I hadn't left my house until late afternoon I'm not surprised, but it is annoying to try and navigate the desolate highway that is poorly lit. My eyes feel heavy and my head is pounding with my hangover. I should stop, eat and sleep for a while. I know there is a motel coming up– I'll check in, grab drive- thru food and take it in the room with me then catch some sleep.

The motel looks exactly like I remember it, a run- down row of rooms on either side of the pot- holed parking lot. The brightly lit office sits behind a floor to ceiling wall of windows. As I pull up, I can see the clerk– a red headed girl about twenty. She sets her book down as the door chimes my entrance.

"How you doin' tonight?" she asks in a friendly tone.

"Pretty good, now," I say, noticing her chest as she stands behind the tall counter top.

She smiles and gives me a look that says she appreciates the view as well.

"You got a room for me?" I sidle up to the tall desk and rest my elbows on top of the cool top.

"Sure do."

"Great, I'll just need it for the night." She hands me a key, it has the number 12 engraved neatly into it.

"You have one closer to the office?" Since I have my eye on her anyway I'd like to see where this could go.

"Number one is open, it's right next door."

"I'd like that one."

She gets that key and has me sign a log in book. After collecting the money, she hands me the key.

"I'm going out for some food, could I bring you something?"

"Oh, you don't have to do that. I'm off in an hour– I could just get something on my way home."

"How about I go get us something and you come eat it with me?"

She giggles, and sucks her lip into her mouth, dragging her teeth as it makes its way back out. I can see that she will accept my offer, maybe before she knows, so I ask her what she likes.

"I'll just have whatever you're having, and a chocolate shake." It sounds like she's asking if that's alright, and I think it's adorable that she is shy. It makes me want to make her let loose and get free of that.

"I'll be waiting for your knock then. Kelly. I add after reading it from the nametag she has pinned to her top.

"Ok, Tyler." She must have read it before because she doesn't look away from my eyes to confirm it with the paper I've signed. I'm surprised that it was possible for her to make out my chicken scratch signature.

I leave with her watching my back as I walk out. I can see in the reflection of the windows that her eyes never leave my ass. I smirk at her audaciousness.

I unlock the door to my room; the straight out of the 70's style décor hits me right away. The mustard yellow bedspread and avocado carpeting clashing just like the good 'ol days. It hasn't been remodeled to look retro either, this is very much original to the period.

The shower looks like its seen better days and those days were decades ago. I strip out of my clothes and take a chance with the germs permeating the filth in the stall and stand under the hot stream, washing away the night of drinking and the hours of driving.

I feel refreshed– and slightly disgusted– as I wrap a stiff towel around my waist. I shake my head, flinging water droplets all over the mirror and let my shaggy hair dry naturally, as it's what looks best on me.

After dressing, I grab my keys and head back out, making sure I have the room key to let myself back in. I killed most of the hour in the shower so I rush to the 24-hour drive thru of the closest burger joint. The night is cool and I crack the windows slightly to enjoy the night's air.

I come back to the room and set the bags of food down on the circular table with two chairs. I kick off my shoes and get comfortable in one of them and not a full minute later the knock on the door excites me.

"Come in," I tell her, having left the door unlocked in anticipation for her.

It opens a crack and then slowly reveals her standing there on the other side. She looks even better now that I can see all of her. Her tiny waist makes her tits look even bigger in her tight black tank top– she's not wearing a bra, so I can see the hard nipples not hidden underneath. The tattoos along her arms, I hadn't seen before, hiding under a light sweater she conveniently left somewhere else. Her round ass hugged tightly by her skinny jeans.

Fuck, she's going to be a good time.

"All the way in."

She looks like she's only just realized she hasn't exactly entered the room. "Oh." She joins me at the table, going right for the shake I put in front of her food. "Thank you," she says after taking a hard pull on the straw, the effort sucking her cheeks in.

"Dig in." I'm starving now, the room full of the smells of fattening food and the hot red head sitting across from me– who's *totally* willing to fuck, tantalizing all my senses.

I unwrap my burger and take a huge bite, it only makes me hungrier, I hadn't realized just how ravenous I'd let myself become.

I watch her as she eats– much more slowly than me, and when I'm done I just sit and stare. It would seem creepy for a man who is not me– who doesn't look like I do, but I'm able to get away with it. I've been described as 'hot' more times than I can count and when I look in the mirror I can be happy with what I see. My deep blue eyes and blond hair that frames a chiseled jaw, lightly dotted with fuzz. Full lips women enjoy kissing and a tight muscular body they love to get their hands on.

I don't look away when she catches my eyes, she dares to hold my stare but is unable to for any length of time. She's trying to be daring– it's adorable.

I finally speak, pulling myself from my imagination. "You're fucking beautiful, you know that?" I mean it, she really is stunning.

She laughs, not like the giggles I've heard come from her, but a real from- the- gut laugh and it makes me laugh.

"Thank you," she says when she remembers her manners.

"Do you have someone who will be wondering about you?"

She gives me a look I can't name and says, "Why? Are you planning on doing something horrible to me?"

She's joking, I can tell, but I see it become a realization to her quickly. I laugh and tell her I have nothing untoward planned for her. "I only want what you want."

"And what is that?" she says flirtatiously.

"You want me to tell you what *you* want or what *I* want?" I ask, pulling myself to the end of my chair.

"What do you think I want?"

I put my hands on her knees and push them apart until they are stopped by the armrests of the chair. "First, I think you want me to run my hands up your thighs until I can feel the heat coming from your little pussy." Her gasp tells me I'm on the right track. "Then you want me to drag your pants down your legs and bury my face inside of you."

She doesn't stop me when I get on my knees in front of her, so I go about doing what I've said, reaching for her zipper, I slide it down slowly. I grab the waistband of her pants and tug them down; she lifts her ass to help me. I pull off her shoes to get rid of her pants completely.

She tries to bring her legs back together, probably feeling exposed, but I don't let her. I put one leg on either of the wooden armrests and look at her glistening slit. I blow slowly on it watching her reaction to me. Her nipples are hard and her breath is coming heavy.

"You want me to taste this beautiful pussy of yours?"

I wait for her to answer, it takes longer than I think it should, but she finally nods and that is all the confirmation I need to dive in there. I slide my tongue up her cleanly shaven lips.

God she tastes delicious.

I dip my tongue inside her and lap it up. She moans loudly when I reach her clit, sucking it into my mouth hard and then tickling it with my tongue, alternating gentle and hard– it drives her crazy. I pull back when I feel her tightening for her orgasm only to bring her to that point again moments later.

My cock is harder than it has been in a long while, I can't wait to get in to her delicious cunt. I push my fingers inside and the tightness of her hole grips my digits, I have to make a real effort to fuck her with them.

I lift her top with my other hand and bare her tits to me. Perfect, like I knew they would be– full and perky with soft pink nipples that are hard from being turned on while fucked. I pull one into my mouth and her already tight pussy clenches tighter around my fingers. "God, your pussy is like a vice grip." I say, switching sides, giving the same attention to her other tit. She arches her back and her hips start working in tandem with my fingers to get her off.

I put my mouth back onto her clit and I finally let her come. Before Kelly has a chance to recover, I pick her up off the chair and toss her onto her back on the bed– she scoots into the center of the mattress with her elbows and spreads herself for me, again.

I undress slowly, letting her watch as I reveal myself to her. She squirms with excitement, waiting patiently for me to fuck her.

"Now, you want me to put my cock inside of you. Don't you?"

She nods.

I take my hard dick in my hand and stroke it in front of her, alleviating the ache that had grown from ignoring it. I slide a condom on and climb in between her legs, pushing her knees up to her ears as I go– folding her in half. Then I line us up and push the full length of my cock into her, giving her no time to become accommodated with the girth, I start fucking her deep.

Her panting and yelps are being cut off by the next cry. She sounds like a porn star, but I know she's not faking. I can see in her face the pain of having me inside her at this angle– with this relentless rhythm. She is enjoying herself– the wet sounds coming from her pussy are enough proof of that.

I tip her ass up off the mattress scooting underneath her, resting the back of her thighs on top of my bent knees then drag her up by her arms sitting her on my lap– never breaking our connection.

She rides me, bouncing fast enough to get her tits jiggling. "Fuck, you look good." I say, gritting my teeth.

She likes the compliment, flipping her long hair over her shoulder so I can see more of her chest, which is what I wanted. I lean in and trap one of her nipples between my teeth, biting harder than is comfortable, but she doesn't pause, if anything it makes her more hungry for my dick.

I take the length of her hair in my fist and pull her head back exposing her neck, which I slide my tongue along until I move her mouth to mine, forcing her lips open with my tongue; I fuck her mouth. She kisses me back with my same hunger. We're not moving with any sort of rhythm– both just needing to fuck and be fucked.

I flip her over, "Get on your knees."

She does what I tell her, round ass in the air– at this angle it looks even bigger and more round. Her tight little ass hole calling to me but I don't want to have that conversation right now, I just want to nut inside of her.

I stand at the end of the bed and drag her toward me, pushing my way into her wet hole. I pull her up by her hair– her back flush with my front– and I thrust into her, resuming the frantic pace from before.

"Touch your pussy." I whisper into her ear.

She does as she's told and I feel her fingers work her pussy quickly, bumping into my cock occasionally from the frantic way she's rubbing her clit.

"I want to feel your orgasm, I want your pussy so wet it drips down your thighs." I thrust deeper, slapping our skin together.

I use her tits as a grip hold to keep her in place as I fuck her for my own release, quick and hard. I feel as soon as she reaches hers, holding my cock tightly, the friction is enough to do it for me. I pump everything I have into the condom and bite my teeth into her neck to muffle my groan.

I slide out of her, my cock misses her warmth instantly. She flops forward onto her stomach and I climb up next to her to lie down myself. I take the fully loaded condom off and toss it in the direction of the trash. I'm sure I didn't make it inside but I don't have enough energy to care. I wrap an arm around her waist, pulling her against me; my hand falls to her ass. I give it a squeeze.

She moans.

I smile.

I fall asleep before I realize I'm going to.

Chapter Four

I awaken sometime in the early morning hours inside of her again. She must have taken it upon herself to take advantage of my morning wood. Both of us are on our sides, her ass is grinding into me. I feel right away that I don't have a condom on but that can't stop me now.

She must realize I am finally awake because she starts moving quicker, backing her ass into me. She feels so good unsheathed– so wet and warm, too late, now to worry about the consequences.

I pull her up onto my lap, facing away from me. I watch her round ass jiggle as she fucks me, mesmerized by my thick cock going in and out of her tight hole.

I suck my thumb into my mouth to wet it and without warning push it inside of her tight ass hole. It drives her wild, she fucks me fast and hard, milking my cock until it's spurting inside of her and she comes seconds later, falling back onto me.

"I'm on the pill," she says by way of an answer to that question that was right on my tongue to ask.

I rub my hands up and down her tummy, loving the feel of her covering me. I cup her tits and pull her nipples hard between my fingers.

"I should get cleaned up," she says and tries to leave.

I roll her off me and push her back into the mattress, spreading her legs. "I want to see my come inside of you."

She bites her lip, that fucking lip that makes me want to fuck her mouth. She spreads her thighs apart and I can already see the creamy white dripping from her hole.

"*Fuck,* it looks good in there." I push my fingers inside of her and work them around, smearing my come across her slick pussy after taking them out. Then I tell her she can go get cleaned up.

She goes shyly to the restroom, coming out a few minutes later looking a little less fucked, although still completely naked, she walks over to her clothes and gets dressed. "Check out is at 11:00," she says

"I'll be out before then," I say back.

"Ok."

And she fucking leaves– just like any good whore, she's out before it gets weird.

Fuck, I'll miss her.

I want to go back to sleep but I don't let myself, I need to get back on the road. I take a shower instead. I change into a fresh pair of jeans and a new tee, slip into my shoes and do a quick glance around the room, making sure I haven't forgotten anything.

I drop the key at the office with an old man I'm glad wasn't here to check me in last night, it wouldn't have been nearly as fun a night if he had. He asks me about my stay and I tell him it did the job.

I get back on the road, stopping at a coffee shop to grab a large cup for the road and make quick work of it during the next leg, stopping once for food, which I eat as I drive.

I see the lights of the town just as night falls. The familiar glow of my hometown brings about memories I had forgotten along the way.

I call the attorney's number back and let Mr. James know that I've arrived. He tells me to go ahead and come up, that he will be in his office.

I do just that as I come to the familiar building, which has changed a lot yet somehow remained the same, the rustic red brick colored façade now covered over with a white washed paint, giving it an updated look in this grungy town. He must do fairly well for himself here. A brightly lit sign adorning the entry leads the way.

He has me sit down before starting his spiel. "Mr. Rydek, again, I'm so sorry for your loss."

"It's fine, I'm fine, let's just get on with this. I've had a long drive and I just want to get to my parent's house and settle in for the night."

His expression tells me I've been too blunt so I ease up on him. He has also lost a good friend in my father– so he says.

"I'm just going to read his last wishes for you. Then you can be on your way."

"Great," I say, leaning into the chair, settling in for what I imagine is going to take a while.

"Basically, your father has left you everything, the house and all its contents. The car lot– he would really like it if you would run it. He says here if you'd rather not he would like you to sell it and use the money for something useful, not to throw it away."

I roll my eyes; I can practically hear my father in those words. He had always been so worried about where my money goes. Which is ridiculous– I've never given him any reason to think I'm a frivolous spender. I own my house outright and my college loans have never been in default. I'd never asked the man for a dime.

But, he had come from a family that was scraping by most times with a drunken father who'd plundered most of his earnings, so I let it slide, knowing he meant well. "Is that it?" I ask, trying to mask my irritation.

"He's left a large sum of money from a life insurance policy. $250,000. That will be yours to do with as you see fit."

The money sounds good to me; although I'm sure my money hungry mother will think I should do something for her with it. "Did he have one for my mother as well?"

"I have you labeled soul beneficiary."

Well, that gives her even more reason to hate me. My father never really liked her, even as a child I could tell he wasn't fond of her– her bitching and complaining about any and all things he did drove him away even before I left. Her incessant nagging pushed us both away. Only he had stayed for whatever reasons he thought outweighed the life he'd have without her. Now he's gone and never gets a second alone without her, I'm sad he never got away. As bad as that sounds, it's more truth than anything I've ever thought.

"Great," I say, and even I can hear that it sounds like a bad idea for him to have done.

"He restored three vintage cars; those titles will be transferred over to you, and the contents of a safe deposit box he held at the bank here in town."

I know the one he's talking about– it being the only bank in town, I assume it's where everyone has to do their banking business. "What's in that?" I ask.

"The contents are not labeled– I have no idea." He hands me a key along with the paper he'd been reading and reiterating to me. I look it over and see that he has missed nothing.

"Is that everything, then?"

"Yes it is. Thank you for coming on such short notice. I know it must be a hard time for you. Your father was a great man. I'm sure you know that though."

"I do, absolutely. Thank you for staying late to see me tonight. I appreciate your time."

"Not a problem at all, it was nice to finally meet you, your father had nothing but kind words when speaking of you."

"I'm sure that's true, he never spoke of the bad things about anyone. Thanks again." I fold the paper, sticking it into my back pocket and leave before he can rope me into one of those 'remembering the good old times' conversations.

It's too late to go to the bank tonight, I'll have to make that trip tomorrow. I head in the direction of my old house. Something I'd never thought I'd do again, unless of course my father died… but only then.

I'm surprised the house is dark when I pull up, my mother never kept late hours but I had assumed she'd wait for me to get here. I don't ring the bell, I grab the key I know to be under the fake rock in the flower bed by the door and head inside.

It looks as it always has– like my drunk mother decorated, nothing really going together or fitting in the space it was intended for. I never did like the look of this place. It has great potential, being an old farmhouse style layout, long and brick, with a wraparound patio area around the entirety of the bottom story- the brick whitewashed and beautiful but when you walk inside it's a huge contradiction.

Since it's mine now, I have a quick thought of gutting the whole thing and starting over. I could really turn this into something great. But I have my fucking mother to worry about now. Where the fuck would I put her? I don't know what my father may have done to ensure she would be ok without him, nor do I care really, other than how it will affect me. Which is an awful thing to say about the woman who gave me life, but I can assure you if she were your mother you'd have the same thoughts. This is one fucked up woman to grow up with.

I look around the rest of the bottom floor before heading up to my old room, no sign of my mother anywhere. I walk past their– her– bedroom but the door is closed and I don't really think I'm ready to see her yet, so I let her be. I catch myself actually tiptoeing past the door; I must really be dreading the sight of her.

I push the door closed quietly and flip the light on; throwing my bag on the bed, I look around. It all looks as I last left it. It feels like I'm 16 again, which is the last time I'd done anything in here to spruce it up. The half- naked pictures of women I'd jacked off to hung on the walls next to more trophies than I ever had room for.

I'd always been into sports, learning early on that the girls always wanted the boys that played. And I wanted the girls. I liked to play, don't get me wrong, but the incentives were better than the actual sport. I was good at most things I put my mind to, sports came easy, then the girls came even easier.

I flip on the TV just for background noise. I text Cammie, letting her know I made it. Then I call her a few minutes later when I don't get a response. "Cam... where the fuck are you? I could use a little comfort right now, my fucking dad just died. What the fuck are you doing that's more important than that?" I leave those words as a message on her voicemail and fling my phone onto the bed.

I get undressed and slip into the covers; my parents have always kept the thermostat a tad too cold in this house.

I fall asleep quickly, still not having caught up on my sleep with this whole ordeal.

Chapter Five

I wake early, it's still dark out, but the birds tell me it's morning, I haven't been woken by nature sounds in a long time. It's actually nice. I've finally replenished my missing sleep, I can feel it in my bones. The weariness is gone and my brain is able to focus despite the dreams of younger me being home, the times I try hard not to remember, the times my mother was not a mother, but the devil.

The urge to pee is what finally has me up and out of bed. I relieve myself and plop back onto the mattress, arms tucked behind my head I let my mind wander to the girl at the motel. *Fuck*, she was cute. Maybe I'll stay there on the way back. Maybe get into that tight little ass next time, she had enjoyed my finger in there, little ass slut.

Her perfect tits come to mind and make me hard again. I'm not usually a chest man, but those were perfect, and they had bounced like mad while she had ridden my dick. I tug my cock a few times before I stop myself. Although I'd love nothing more than to leave a nut stain right across the sheets I don't give into that urge, instead I wrap my hand around my cock unmoving until I feel it softening. Focusing my thoughts on the impending errands I need to get done today– starting with the bank, I need to get over there and get the contents of my father's box. I should do that before my mother wakes so I don't have to see her first thing this morning.

I dress quickly and sneak past her still- closed door.

Relief floods when she is not downstairs. I leave quickly, climbing into the car and heading for thc bank, I'm curious to see what my father had kept in there, I knew nothing of a safe deposit box, I didn't even know my father to be the type to keep one.

The town, overall, looks as I remember, old and a little run down, full of mom and pop shops run by the town's residences, the two stop lights are still functioning and no more have been added. I guess the population hasn't grown enough to warrant an additional one. If I'm being honest, I don't remember a time I actually used the stop lights as they were intended, more like a stop sign, just double check no one – or police, are coming and just drive on through. Anyone around here knows that to be how they work, people even stop at the green lights to make sure the person with the red light did not have the right of way.

I pull into the empty bank parking lot, for having the business of the entire town, it's not as busy as everyone might assume.

I reach for my cell and call Cammie, she's really pissing me off now, why the fuck won't she answer? I call four times before giving up and texting her that she needs to get ahold of me. *Bitch*. I toss the phone into the passenger seat and head for the entrance of the bank.

Andrea, who I went to school with, is the teller that calls me over. "Hey," she says in a too-chipper voice. The girl always had a crush on me, like, in a way that creeped me out and never let me fuck and use her. I kept far away from her, her chubby body helped with the task. She looks better now, trimmed down, but her face is still that of the girl that I recall watching my every move and asking me to every dance that the school held. Overtly throwing herself at me at every party we found ourselves at together.

"Hey, Andrea," I say and a shock crosses her face, maybe she was expecting me not to recall her name, but one does not simply forget their stalkers names– or faces.

"Oh, my god, you look so good, Tyler… I mean you have always looked so good, but now you're a man."

Oh my fuck, some things never change.

"Thanks," I say with a small smile so as not to piss her off and make her go crazy stalker on me. I don't add anything about how she looks.

She asks what brought me in and I'm assuming she knows about my father because it's a small town and everyone knows your business, sometimes even before the person the news is about knows. I've found out plenty of things about me and my family through the grapevine rather than actual facts from the sources.

"Just here to collect my father's safe deposit box's contents. Could you help me out with that?" I say it a little nicer than I need to, in case it's a hassle or too much work, she may be able to expedite the process.

"I'm so sorry for your loss, I always remember you two having such good times together." The look of pity on her face makes me want to hit her. I shake that from my mind and the fact that she was not an invited witness to any happy times with my father. You think she'd want to hide the fact that she stalked me, but instead she uses that information to recall 'memories' of me.

"I'm fine, thanks for saying that." What the fuck does a person say when people are apologizing for things they've had no part in? *Whatever.* "Think you could help me out with that box?" I hold the key up to help her focus… maybe she likes shiny things.

"Oh, sure, follow me."

I do, and as we reach the rows of boxes, she grabs for my arm and waits until I look at her before she speaks. "You want to get a drink or something?" She attempts a flirty smile, but it looks like a sneer and it's not flattering, luckily I have an excuse this time and it is air tight.

"I'm just not ready to be social right now, you know, losing my dad sure did a number on me.

Thanks for the offer though, maybe another time." I wink at her, I don't know why. I can pretty much hear the rush of wet flood her panties. I almost laugh. The whimper that escapes her does finally make me laugh. I don't mask it. I don't wonder if I've hurt her feelings– I just want his over with,

She hands me a metal box without another word and won't make eye contact again, the submissive thing works for her. I could do some things to *this* Andrea– and not nice things, well, not for her. I hold back that laugh, unlike what you might think, I'm not usually a dick.

"Thanks," I say, taking the box from her and setting it on the table. I open it with more eager curiosity than a Christmas present. It looks like a shit ton of paper work mostly, there is some jewelry and trinkets in here that look like they've meant something along the way. I don't remember them all. Most are my grandmother's things, I remember her wearing many of the pieces.

The rewritable CD that I see is confusing more than anything so far. I don't think of my dad as much of a tech guy. Not even techy enough to make a disk, I'll have to check out his efforts. I think maybe he's converted photos to disk. It might be interesting to look back at some of those times, even if they are not fond memories.

I take the paperwork out and dump the rest of the contents onto the table then load up my pockets with what will fit. Andrea must think I look foolish– mostly because I do. I should have brought something to carry this shit, but I hadn't thought about the fact that my father would be sentimental or a mild hoarder.

I thank Andrea for her help, not waiting for a response and head for my car, emptying the contents of my pockets into the seat next to me. I'll take them into the house when I get back.

I check my phone, no response from Cammie. I think about texting her something mean– more mean than I've already been to her. Maybe breaking it off, but I don't, instead, I head back home, stopping first for a breakfast sandwich that I eat in the driveway before going in. Whether my mother has cooked something is not of my concern, she has always been an awful cook in the kitchen. I'd have passed on her concoction either way.

I go inside finally, taking a deep breath to ready myself for seeing her; she will definitely be up now, although when I don't see her downstairs I get a little excited to put off this reunion for a while longer. I decide to check through the rest of the house, calling to her, although I'm not eager to see her, the trepidation is killing me, better to get it over with rather than dwelling on it, I suppose.

"Mom," I call throughout the upper level. I knock on her bedroom door when I reach it, turning the handle when she does not answer.

The room is dark; the shades are drawn. I can't see the bed clear enough to say one way or the other if she is tucked inside, so I go forward. It's empty. She must have gone out. Relief floods, along with something else I can't name right now– something close to regret, even though she was an awful, selfish, whore of a woman she is still my mother and maybe a little comfort from her right now would be nice. She has never been type to hug the sadness away, leaning more toward the 'oh, fuck he's crying again, I better avoid him' side. It might be nice to see if there has been a change in the way she might handle such things now that I am older.

I sit on the end of the bed. The room is so fucking flowery and feminine; my father never put much effort into fighting for what he wanted. 'Just let your mother have her way, it's just easier,'– that was his motto. It made me so angry to hear; knowing my mother took full advantage of that frame of thought– took full advantage of most things in this fucking house. I get angry with her all over again. She is such an awful woman.

I'm angry at my father for letting her win all of the time, it taking away my own choices in most matters. Forcing me to sit by and let her do whatever she wanted, not backing me up and helping me stand up to her.

My life would have been far better if she were not involved and now I wish it was her being buried in a few days. I'm angry at her for not letting my father live a single day without her and her demanding ways.

I leave the room and slam the door shut behind me, rattling the walls.

Fucking bitch.

My anger rearing its ugly head, anger I'd somehow tricked myself into thinking was behind me.

I have to be here through the day of the funeral, I'm not going to miss that just to avoid my mother. I think four more days of this sneaking around will not be too hard to handle knowing there is an end to it.

I'll just let her stay in the house until she meets her own fate and then sell it. Then we won't have to have that awkward talk about where she might live or how she would afford it. I don't even want to talk about the fact that my father has left me everything.

He had inherited this house from his family and my mother must not have gotten on the deed if he can hand it over to me outright without her permission. It's actually a shame that the house would leave the family. I may keep it after all, not to live in, but to pass down if I have children. I almost laugh at the thought of me fathering a kid, it's not likely, but who can say what the future holds.

I'm only 25, I can't know what will come down the line in a few years. I'm guessing nothing too much further with Cammie if she can't even be bothered to call me now. But, there is a world of women out there that may love to come when I call. The thought excites me, having some submissive girl begging me to tell her what to do and fucking her silly.

Fuck.

That would be perfect; I think I may end it with Cammie after all. She would never be that. She practically makes me work for her pussy and it's often times not worth the effort.

I only had to lay a fast food meal in front of the motel girl, Kelly, and she road my cock like a fiend and nothing was awkward with her, little effort for massive reward. I like that.

I go about unpacking my bag, getting a little more settled in, I wonder where my mother had run off to this morning. She hadn't left a note telling me what she may be up to. I know she didn't have a meeting with that attorney. Maybe the grocery store?

I call Cammie one more time, "We need to talk, I feel like wc need to have a good heart to heart and this avoiding me shit has gone too far. Call me. Now!" I leave on her voicemail.

My phone buzzes before I put it down. A text. "We have nothing more to talk about."

What the fuck? Women and their fucking mind trips. "What are you talking about?" I hit send.

"You have some really big balls to think I'd want anything to do with you after what you did."

Well, I know she has no idea what I do. She has no idea about the women I fuck behind her back or the things I love to do to them. "Where's this coming from?" I feign innocence.

"Are you fucking serious?" She never swears, not so much as a 'damn', so I know something must really be bothering her.

"I don't have any idea what could have gotten your panties in a bunch. Please remind me of this awful thing I've done."

"Goodbye."

I hit call and wait for her to answer, she sends me to voicemail instead. "You fucking call me, or you'll regret it." I don't know what I'll do if she doesn't, but this fucking mind fuck has got to stop, I *will* have the upper hand. "You have until tomorrow to have a normal conversation with me." I hit end angrily.

Nothing comes from her end, but I don't really expect it right away, she will wait until the deadline before responding. I know her well. I tuck the phone in my pocket and head for the kitchen. I need another cup of coffee. Then I'll get my hands on that disk, see what my dad thought important enough to save.

The coffee is dark and delicious; I take it up to my room and put the unlabeled disk into my laptop, as the images flood the screen I realized it was not meant for me.

My father is ass naked, leaning over the table in what looks like the basement, pushing buttons on his recording device and setting the frame up. As soon as he steps away from view, I see my mother equally naked. It sends shivers across my body. I've seen her in this exact way countless times– spread eagle and waiting. I can almost hear her voice now, 'such a good boy, come love your mother.' That old familiar feeling of dread hits me in the pit of my stomach. For some reason I continue to watch. That is how fucked up she's made me.

He walks over to her and starts to fuck her. She doesn't move, much like a dead fish, just lets him fuck her. She is soundless as well, which as I recall is unlike her. She was always very vocal with me when she made me fuck her.

He goes at her vigorously; I've never seen them together like this. I know most kids wouldn't, but in my house, with a whore of a mother like I had, you'd think she would have liked having me catch her being fucked– try and make me jealous or some shit. The mind games I've encountered my whole life started with her. But I avoided a closed door like the plague, not wanting any more of her than I was forced in to.

My father's ass cheeks clench and unclench as he works her over. I'm not able to look away. I wish I could, the memories of myself standing where my father is now, between her legs, come flooding in– although it was never in the basement.

She loved me to come in her room at night when my father would work late. I'm not at all sure he was unaware of what was happening. How could he not have known though?

She loved living on the edge of almost being caught, loved to push the envelope. Calling me in only a few minutes before he was due home, insisting I fuck her, rubbing herself in front of me, knowing it worked to turn me on and make me hard. Rubbing me through my pants to make sure it happened. Being at a young and impressionable age, it worked effortlessly. She took advantage of teenage hormones and used them in her favor. She would suck me off in the garden after insisting I help her with the plants– my father in the house just a few feet away. She was my first at everything and insatiable with her demands. She couldn't get enough of me.

I watch while my father finishes, pulling out, I can't see much but his arm is pumping his cock aimed right over her mound. The first real sound comes as he grunts while coming. Then he leans over and grabs a towel, wiping his spunk from her.

She still has not engaged. Even as he walks away to stop the recording she says nothing, just lies there. She never would have been like that with me. For some reason I take that as a win on my behalf. Some fucked up part of me has counted that as a victory. I fucked my mother better than her husband– my father did.

Woo fucking hoo. I am disgusting. *Thanks mom.*

I'm about to push the eject button, assuming that must be it, a simple recording for the spank bank for my father's keepsake, but another scene of my father in the same nakedness leaning over the camera, fixing settings for the video stops me.

I watch as he goes to my mother again, this time her ass is in the air, down on all fours. I remember her loving that. She loved it from behind. Her legs are wide and this time the camera is closer, my father doesn't last as long as the first time. He finishes quickly, after going at her hard and fast.

This time as he pulls out to come I notice how wide my mother's pussy is– it's gaping, a perfect circle right through to her insides. I'm bigger than my father, cock and all… by a lot and I've never made her hole look like that, even after she made me fuck her with larger objects, her hole accommodating most anything she thought of. Her pussy always returned to normal after it was out.

My father must be working her over quite a bit. Maybe it's because her pussy is shaved, that's new, she always kept a little hair on there. Maybe it was always like that and I missed it, I doubt it… but it could be.

He wipes off the come he emptied onto her then goes to the camera to turn it off and this time another scene does not follow.

I don't want it to be true but my cock, which I've been ignoring, is achingly hard. Most people would be disgusted watching what I just had– their parents fucking, but my mother did quite a number on me, and my father fucking her was not as disgusting as I thought it would be to see.

Fuck.

I squirm in my seat, trying to situate my hard cock in a way that I could get comfortable, but unlike the times that I think about women and get hard this isn't going away by simply changing my train of thought. The more I try to ignore it the more I'm reminded that it's there and waiting for me to notice it.

I stand and stretch, hoping the flow of blood reaches other parts of my body, but it is no use, my cock is throbbing so hard I can feel my heartbeat in it. I reach down and do the only thing I can do. I fucking yank on it until I spill my come on the carpet, rubbing it in with my sock covered foot. I don't let myself replay the video, although some part of me wants to– the sicko part that she made for her pleasure. But I don't let her win, not this fucking time. I tuck my cock back into my pants and try not to give the video another thought.

The doorbell rings, interrupting me and I'm not sure what to do. It may be my mother with her hands full of groceries, thinking I should go help her with them. In case that is what's happening I walk slowly down the stairs, not overly excited about seeing her for the first time in this way, especially after watching the video and jacking off for the first time in years because of it.

I calm myself down, gripping the handle of the door; I pull it open unceremoniously, stepping aside to let her in. Only it's not her. It's Jamie, a flood of memories, all including her naked and sprawled out in front of me– the cock- hungry whore who would do anything for me at the drop of a dime. "Jamie," I say, looking at her from head to toe.

Nice.

"Hi, Tyler," she says as hungry for me as ever.

Fuck, I just might have to get in this. "What's up?"

"I just thought I'd stop by and see if you need… me." She licks her lips seductively.

"Fuck, baby, I just might." My cock jumps, thinking about her tight little pussy wrapped around me. "Come in."

She smiles at me, walking past and then stands behind me.

"You seen my mom in town today? Don't know where she is at the moment."

"No, I haven't seen her for a while." She comes up to me rubbing her hands down my chest, brazenly grabbing hold of my jean covered cock. "Does that mean we have the house to ourselves?"

"I guess it does. Why don't you go on up to my room and get naked."

She does without a word, stripping as she goes.

I follow her up, taking my own clothes off as well.

"Get the fuck on the bed."

"Oh my god, my pussy has missed you so fucking much. Nothing makes me come like your massive dick."

"Put your ass up." I come up quickly behind her, spreading her cheeks apart to see her ass hole–my favorite thing about her. Her ass is always so hungry for my dick.

"You gonna let me in this hole?" I push my thumb against the entrance; it gives only a little.

"Anything you want. Take whatever you want." Her pussy is so wet; it glistens as I manipulate her back hole.

Music to my fucking ears.

I look into the side table at my bed and see that the lube bottle that has been in there since last time I used it is still there, right where I left it. I squeeze a small amount into my fingers then rub it into her puckered hole and down her pussy crack and then I push three fingers into her hungry hole. The wetness seeping from her pussy mixes with the lube, aiding in the effort.

She moans loudly and greedily tells me, "more." So I give her more, adding my remaining digits into her juicy hole. She yelps when I slide into her up to my wrist and then she grinds her hips against me.

I push the thumb from my other hand into her ass and she goes crazy. Last time we fucked, I wasn't even eighteen yet, I've learned a few things since then.

Try as I might, I can't get the video out of my head. Although I don't want it there it drives me forward, making me so fucking hard– harder than I would be normally doing such things. I try to get angry with myself for it but that emotion won't come, instead I embrace it. I fuck her fast with my fist until she comes so hard her pussy squirts– that's not uncommon for her, she has always been a squirter.

I take my hand out of her and it's covered in her cream, I use it to stroke my cock to get it ready for her ass which I enter as I would a pussy, hard and relentless. I push against her ass's rejection and I fuck her tight hole as it squeezes me almost painfully.

If this were any other girl she'd be crying right now, but this one is unlike the rest, she loves this. *Craves it.* And I'm more than happy to oblige. It's been more time than I'd like since I've ripped into an ass hole and what better way to welcome me back to it than this girl.

"Oh, fuck, Tyler. *Fuck me.*"

I go at her harder than usual, I have to grip her tightly and pull her back against me to stop her from falling forward. Our skin slapping so hard together that it's turning hers a light shade of red. She is yelping and making nonsensical gibberish as confirmations for my efforts.

"I want you to come inside my ass."… "Fill up my hole."

That's what I can make from her, she's spewing all sorts of porn star phrases at me. It fuels me, I want to rip her in half with my cock, tear her open and come inside of her deeper than I have ever done.

I pump her until I my balls are ready to explode and when they do, I push into her deeply and fill her up as requested.

I pull out of her and she keeps her ass up for me but the rest of her body collapses onto the bed. I can't help but look inside of her, I've always been drawn to the holes I've come inside. There is a ring of white cream around her ass hole and I rub it into the red hole.

She whimpers, I can't imagine her ass not being sore.

Poor little slut.

I spread her open and peer inside.

Fuck it looks good in there. I love the thought of my come sitting inside of her ass, oozing from her after it warms.

"Your ass is so full." Even though I came only minutes before she showed up, I still had plenty to give her.

My mother did that for me, conditioned me to be always ready and hungry for more. I'm sure Jamie would thank her if she knew, she has been on the receiving end of my cock– letting me have plenty of use out of this hole, more than any other woman in this entire town.

Aside from good 'ol mom, she would never be in second place, she had far more years with me than any other woman.

When I'm finished admiring her asshole, which is now tightly closed, I tell her she can get up.

"Is there anything else I can do for you?"

I couldn't imagine what else she could have in mind, our interactions have never been more than me ordering her into a position and then fucking her. We've never even had a conversation about anything outside of sex.

"No, I think that really helped, I had a bunch of things to work out and your ass has helped immensely." To any other girl that may have been insulting, but not her, she takes it as permission to be done here.

"Ok, then, call me if you want me again before you leave. I'll be around."

"I will." I know that to be true, no way would I leave this town not hitting that again.

I show her out, she walks a little like she's just been on a horse– her ass must really hurt. I know my balls feel like they've taken a beating, smashing them into her ass has made them tender.

I go back upstairs, having come down completely naked, I don't have to undress to climb into the shower. I don't give it much thought, I know my mother could have been home after the time Jamie and I had spent in there. I can't help but think I wanted her to see I'd taken another woman into my room and made her howl like a virgin in a horror movie being torn to shreds from the inside out.

She may have been jealous, although she hadn't initiated things with me for a few months before I had left. I'd always wondered what made her stop. I kept waiting for her to call to me and when she didn't I was relieved at first, then I was curious as to what may have made her change her mind about me.

I had this routine, well, my cock did. I went elsewhere fucking any hole that would let me inside, making my way through every girl who had ever looked my way, from my friend's mothers, to anyone who gave me that 'come fuck me' look.

I'd had other girls while my mother was using me, but she took up most of my time and then I didn't have that as an outlet so I needed to fill her demanding schedule, one she forced me to keep as well, with other women. No one ever being as hungry as her for cock, I had to have many girls in the mix.

Chapter Six

I shower quickly, dressing in clean clothes. I feel tired, I could probably lie down for a nap right now, but I don't, instead I head for the kitchen, fixing a peanut butter sandwich.

It doesn't look like anyone has been shopping in a while, not much in the pantry to choose from.

I wander around the living room, spotting something out of place almost immediately; the lock on the basement door is new. We never had a master-lock keeping people from opening the door.

There is no access to the house from down there, not even a small window typical in most basements. I recall the small key from the things in the safe deposit box, if I remember right it is a key that could fit this lock.

Tempted by curiosity, more than anything else, I run upstairs for the keys to the car and go retrieve it, along with the rest of the things, putting those on the counter, I bring the key to the lock and sure enough, it works to open it.

It is dark inside, always has been. I wonder if there is some sex swing set up down here, recalling the video of my parents again, my mother sprawled out on the table, maybe they'd upgraded into a real sex dungeon.

I can't turn the overhead light on, it seems to have burnt out, so I pull my phone out of my pocket and turn on the flashlight. It doesn't light up enough to see much, but I take a quick look around, seeing no real reason to warrant the new lock on the door.

It looks a lot like I remember it, the setup is the same: mostly boxes, Christmas decorations from years accumulated, my boxes, stacked neatly in the corner, I'd put them there before I left, promising to come back for what I couldn't take in one trip. I haven't given the contents much thought after packing them– must not be too important. Some old bikes, boxes labeled donations, the now infamous fuck- table covered in a white sheet, probably to keep it dust free for quickies, so they don't have to clean the area first.

I wander over to it and lift a corner, I don't know what compels me, I just simply want to see the spot my father fucked her in the home movie.

Whoa.

I'm shocked to actually see something under the sheet lying on the table. I've lifted only a corner and there is a foot. Toe nails painted red like I remember my mother doing, sometimes soliciting my help, 'come fuck me red' she had called it.

My father has some sex doll under here, I'm sure of it. I almost laugh.

Almost.

Instead, my curiosity forces me to lift it off the rest of the way. Slowly I uncover its knee, then thigh. I go to the other side, doing the same. I'm actually excited to see this, I've thought of getting one of these things. I rub my hand up its inner thigh, stopping just shy of the sheet. It feels smooth. They make them pretty life like, it seems. Next, I reveal the naked pussy, but I can't see it very well with its legs closed.

I continue to pull the sheet higher up, exposing the tits. They're soft and pliable as I can't help but give them each a squeeze. It's a thin looking woman full chested. It has nice flared hips, I'm sure if I flip it over the nice round ass would be there to match.

I reveal the face, I'm curious to see the mouth, I'm sure I'm going to see some sort of apparatus you'd stick your cock into to simulate a blow job. And I am right, but it's on my mother's face. There is a plastic ring encircling its lips, I push my finger into it and the cavity is hollow and ribbed.

How the fuck had he gotten a life sized doll of my mother? And, looking more closely with the flash light I see how remarkable the recreation actually is.

Now that I know what to look for, I can see all the telltale ways this doll meets the standards of being a perfect representation of her. She really has always had a nice body, I can see why he'd gone too all the trouble.

All I can think is she must have stopped letting him fuck her– that this may have even been what he was fucking in the video, I knew my mother couldn't have been that quiet while being fucked.

I can't help myself– I bring the flashlight to the apex of its thighs and the same type of circular hollow cavity is there, two of them, one for the pussy and one for the ass hole. When I run my finger along the circumference of it, my cock does what it would if this were a real woman– my real mother. It fucking hardens.

I want a go at this thing for sure, the faux skin feels soft and the cavity snug, I could really have fun with this but that will have to wait. I can't have my mother coming home knowing her replica brought me to that. That is, if she even knows it exists. She could be the reason for the lock on the door, keeping her on the outs with his little sex- doll secret.

Maybe his little plastic fuck doll mistress is a secret. Sick as it sounds, I may take this thing with me back to my house.

I cover it back up, against my cock's argument that we could get in and out before being caught.

I lock up the door and run up to my room when I don't see any signs of my mother having returned.

And since I've thrown out my no masturbating celibacy I fuck my fist until I come, feeling only mildly satiated, but it does the trick. For now. I'm gonna need to get in that sick little fuck-doll if I'm to alleviate *this* hard- on.

I am having a hard time wrapping my head around my father's need for that little toy. He has my mother here, and although I'm not sure of their sexual habits I can say with first- hand knowledge that, if he wanted it, I'm positive my mother would have no problem opening up for him.

I lie down, exhausted from such a strange day, the realization of the video and what's down in our basement would be mind- fucking enough, but throw in the fact that I literally can't get that sex doll out of my mind, with all its resemblance of my mother set aside… or more possibly because of the uncanny way it is identical to her.

I bet if I replaced the bulb down there and saw it in full light, it would not have such a perfect look to it. It would show the flaws and the missteps in recreation. I close my eyes, I can't hold them open another minute. I fall asleep to the memory of how the doll felt under my fingers, the smooth texture of the skin.

Chapter Seven

There's a noise in the house that awakens me. My eyes pop open, I'm not familiar with my surroundings at first, it takes me a few moments to remember where I am. I realize I've slept until nightfall. The sun hidden away and the moon full in the sky, casting shadows in my childhood bedroom. Familiar shapes forming where they always had. I listen for the sound again, reacquainting myself with memories of this room at night.

I decide to chase down the noise. If it's my mother I'd like to be the one to initiate the meeting to cut down on some of the power she's always held over me.

I walk slowly down the stairs, avoiding the center of the steps where they all creak from age, listening carefully to the silence. I don't hear anything but my beating heart, sending blood rushing into my ears. I realize I'm full of anxiety for the impending reunion.

I crane my neck to look over the banister, hoping to pinpoint where she might be. The room is empty. I rush forward, finishing my descent down the stairs, finally coming to the bottom; I look around only to find nothing that could have been responsible for the sounds I heard.

I'm beginning to think I may have imagined it, possibly something in my dream sounded instead of in reality.

Relieved, I go to the fridge, hungry all of a sudden, it looks the same as this morning; empty. I really hope my mother is stopping at the grocery store tonight. I can only eat so many peanut butter sandwiches before I end up hating them. I devour two, making the second as I eat the first.

As I am taking the last bite of the second one, thinking I may need a third, I notice the papers from my father's safe deposit box on the counter, a diagram drawing my attention.

I thumb through a few of the top ones until I reach the one that had caught my attention. It's of a human outline, words scribbled in my father's handwriting covering the blank spaces around the form. I can't make many of the words out, he's been told a number of times he has the handwriting of a doctor.

I flip to the next; it has his scratchy lettering top to bottom, tiny cursive writing pinched together in the lines of paper. It looks like he was taking notes. The next sheet is the same, endless pages of scribbles. I come to another diagram in the midst of them. This one I can make out a little more clearly.

"disembowel… embalm… preserve…"

What the fuck? It sounds like notes an undertaker would be making.

I turn the page over and continue to try to make out the scattered ramblings. He says something about failed attempts deteriorating before arriving at some sort of sanitation regimen to aid in the preservation– killing off the bad bacterium that initiates decomposition and introducing an exotic cocktail of microorganisms to preserve collagen elasticity and cell structure. He seems to think he may have mastered the recipe.

I didn't know my father was interested in such things. He owned a car dealership, never being the type to open a book, let alone practice things you'd find in medical journals.

The term 'failed attempts' has me wondering what he may have practiced on and what could possibly motivate him to try such things.

Making my way further through the stack I find the recipe, a page headed with the words 'aftercare instructions' with a list detailing the procedure.

-wash with step 1 (follow recipe exactly when reproducing)

-liberally apply step 2 (bottles marked)

-clean cavities thoroughly

The list goes on and is very detailed. I can clearly make out his words here; he seems to have taken extra care in the printing of this sheet. The last thing says to make this a daily chore.

Who has time to complete so many steps... *every* day? And for what? What kind of taxidermist wants to spend countless hours following endless steps to preserve their specimens?

I flip through a few more pages and what catches my attention next is a letter addressed to me.

Tyler,

I know that if you are reading this I'm gone. I want you to know that you have always been my favorite person, I was proud to call you my son.

I had not always been the best father; I know things were not always good for you. I didn't know at the time what your mother was doing to you. I'm sorry I was blind to it. I didn't know I had to be on the lookout for such things. It came to light recently, she felt a strange need to confess. I was shocked. I didn't handle the news well.

That being said your mother is no longer with us. I let the altercation get out of hand and I am at fault for her death. I hadn't told you before this because I couldn't bring myself to admit the truth.

I know you loved her, I know she loved you... a little too much. She shared with me things I cant rid my mind of. She admitted the only reason she stopped sleeping with you was her hysterectomy, there were complications that left her in severe pain on a daily basis.

Since then we were no longer having sex. I was left to my own devices; I had a sort of epiphany. I needed a substitute. A surrogate.

I perfected the process, I'm sure since you've made it this far you've seen the notes, maybe even assumed what I'd been up to. I'm probably not the man you thought you knew while growing up. I've not always been a good man, in my search for a surrogate I'd done awful things to get the right specimen.

What the fuck does he mean by '*specimen*'?

This whole thing has me confused. My father is talking as if he means a *sexual* surrogate. I realize it must have been hard for him after my mother was no longer able to perform in that part of their lives, but what awful things could he have done? I continue reading for the answers.

It came to me one night, lonely and in need of something, I got to thinking. I won't bore you with the details– you can read them for yourself in the notes. I will say that I found a way to preserve the human body so it wouldn't decay. I used that to create a sex doll.

It was through many failed attempts that I arrived at the right process to make it a success. I learned along the way what worked and what had not.

It is simple now looking back; rid the body of the bacteria that feeds on the flesh after death. That was step one– and the hardest. You have the recipe in my notes; you must follow exact measurements.

The bioorganic gel derived from algae was the answer to keeping the bodies soft and malleable after the fat and muscles deteriorated. Injected in just the right spots it's able to keep the shape of the person you are working with.

My 3D printer came in handy to create posable joints capable of locking into place, attached to the major bones, the faux- joints will keep them mobile and flexible to suit your preferences.

Add everything together and you have the perfect woman. I must say that what happened to your mother the night of the fight was a happy accident; I no longer had to search for a new woman. I had her now. I have preserved her. She is in her new home in the basement.

Please don't be alarmed. I don't want to overwhelm you right now. It must be quite a shock to learn all of these things after hearing about my own departure.

I want you to have her.

She is yours now.

What the fuck? The doll downstairs *is* my mother?

I can't breathe.

What is going on here?

My whole life is fucking twisting and I'm not able to see straight.

Not only is my father dead, but my mother is as well. And a fucking sex doll?

To top it off, I can't even be disgusted right now. My stupid fucking aching cock is throbbing, begging me to go back down there and fuck that fucking doll.

I am so fucked, and it turns out, I came from two crazy fuckers who had very little morals to share between them.

What fucking hope did I have?

I read the rest of the letter, resisting the urge to run. To where?– I'm torn between the basement and my home a thousand miles away.

I finish the letter with shaking hands, but I can't tell if the shaking is from disgust or excitement.

Do with her what you will, to be fair she always did what she wanted to you.

I love you son, please don't think of me any differently for this.

If you choose not to accept this gift, I have left a list for you to follow for disposal of her body.

Dad

Chapter Eight

I lay the stack of papers down, my head is swirling and the thoughts trapped inside are confusing and twisted. I know I should be upset that my mother is dead. And I guess I am, but only because I never stood up to her. It sounds like my father did it for me though; he killed her in light of her confession about her depraved appetite for me. I don't know how far she went into detail about what had happened throughout the years, but it was enough to send my father over the edge.

I feel vindicated, and a little angry all at the same time. I feel so dizzy with excitement. I'm so fucked up.

I don't even realize my feet have taken me to the basement door until I reach it. I'm torn between opening the lock right now to use the doll and following my father's list to dispose of her. My shaking hands work the lock. I let my mind wander around the implications of both choices. Of course, my cock wants to weigh in. Of course, the anger at her fuels my perversion, making me want to fuck her silly.

She did this to me, and I wouldn't be held accountable for anything I ended up doing to her, she made me the sex crazed man I am today, the man who is giving real thought to fucking his dead mother, preserved for just such a thing– by his father, no less.

I take a bulb from the lamp in the living room, remembering the one down in the basement is out, after screwing it in light floods the room, sending the shadows to the furthest corners.

The video of my father down here fills my mind as soon as I see the sheet covering her body. The feel of what's under it calling to my hands. I want to touch it again; I want to know it's my mother and really see it for what it is.

I pull the sheet back quickly, whipping it off her body, she looks beautiful, she looks like she is not dead, looks a mixture between sleepy and aroused. I'm sure my father was able to make sure this was how she should be remembered.

I rub my hands up her body.

God, she feels so real.

She feels so soft and I can't get enough of it. She looks just like I remember her; my father hadn't taken any liberties with her– not making one change to enhance her or make her look younger than her 43 years.

She really is beautiful, her dark hair and blue eye combination was coveted by most her girlfriends, her fuller than average lips making her look almost pouty, the straight- lined button- nose with a smattering of light freckles perfectly centered, making her doll- like.

Her porcelain skin preserved perfectly, not a single flaw to ruin the look or feel of her softness, which feels like heaven under my hands. I am compelled to touch her, to spread her.

I'm taken aback by my own actions, watching me do things in a sort of out- of- body way. I watch as my hands run up the inside of her soft thighs, stopping just short of her fleshy mound and back down, the second trip up I don't stop, I can't go another second without touching it.

My fingers are shaking as I touch the folds of my mother's familiar pussy. My cock is achingly hard and pressed against the fly of my jeans, my heart pounding so hard its sending rivers of blood into my ears.

Before I know what I'm doing I push my fingers into the circled cavity. It is warm and tight, it feels like the flesh over the rest of her body, the only difference is this hole has small gripping ribbed bumps the depth of it, I'm assuming he has done it for friction.

I pull my fingers out and then back in again to test my theory. Oh my god, it feels so good. I can't help but imagine my cock is in here instead of my fingers, the grip of this hole would have me coming in no time, and I need that. I need to come so bad right now. My throbbing cock is drooling pre- come in anticipation of what I know I'm going to do.

There is no question anymore.

I let my pants down; they fall heavy to the floor. My feet pull me forward, I stop to spread her legs, true to my father's claims, the locking joints hold her legs up, and open, I stare right into the wide hole I need just before I plunge into it.

I almost explode before I can draw out, I'm like a fucking teenager losing his virginity right now, it's unlike anything I've ever felt.

I am consumed with the thought of this being my mother's existence now. She is here purely for me to fuck at my leisure and the control is overwhelming. Fate has dealt her the hand that she dealt me growing up; I was simply a means to an end for her, to be used as she wanted, when she needed to get off. Now, I would be the one using her and the shear depravity is sending me over the edge.

I slow my shaky breaths, and rest my quivering hands on her breasts, squeezing them at the peak. I move slowly inside her, trying to bring myself to the here and now instead of rushing this, I want to remember it, not look back on it as a blur.

The pussy is practically milking my cock and in only a few more thrusts I can't help but come, I explode harder than I can ever remember doing before. I collapse on top of her, my cock still convulsing inside the ribbed pussy hole, my breath slowing, no longer heaving. The blood is able to flow to other areas of my body.

I don't feel one hint of shame for this, I thought I'd get it out of my system and regret or some other form of self- hating would take over but it doesn't. I'm excited to be the new proud owner of this perfect sex doll.

I pull out of the pussy hole and look for the ribbed tube to pull it out of the socket; my father's instructions told me how to remove them for clean-up. I follow the steps precisely, knowing I want to preserve this fuck doll now, knowing I'll need it for as long as I can think.

I pour some of the solution onto the sleeve and clean it free of my come, leaving it out to air dry.

I pull my pants up finally, after almost tripping over them, still wrapped around my ankles. I take one more look at my new inheritance and head up the stairs before my cock thinks it needs a second round.

Chapter Nine

I had run right up to my room after my interaction with my 'mother' doll, I stayed away physically, but my brain couldn't focus on much else, the excitement swirling around my head was almost constant. I had to take a sleeping pill and go to bed early or I know I would have spent the night in the basement fucking myself dry.

This morning I'm groggy from the pill and exhausted from a night full of weird vivid dreams about my mother, both alive, and the new basement version of her.

I wake to the sound of my phone ringing, still plugged into the wall across the room. As I make my way to it to return the call I missed, I wonder if it's Cammie.

I hope it is Cammie, we have things we need to talk about, like the fact that she *won't* fucking talk to me.

It is her and I hit redial, waiting for her to answer. I hear Cammie's voice right away say hello, she sounds irritated despite the fact that she had been the one to call me.

"Hey, how are you?" I ask, trying hard to start us off on the right foot.

"Fine," she says flatly.

"You missing me?"

She chuffs a laugh, "not really,"

"What the fuck, Cammie? Why can't we just get over this? Why are you being so hard on me?" I spit the words into the phone; this bitch sure can hold a grudge.

"Are you sure you need to ask those questions? You can't just know that what you did to me the night before you left was way too fucked up?" There's more of those swear words she's throwing around lately.

"I do think it was fucked up, but as I tried to explain, it was just that you were so fucking sexy in that little skirt, I got carried away, men sometimes do that when a woman looks sexy, maybe you shouldn't wear that sort of stuff anymore." I know that's not true. If I were a gentleman like she has always thought I was I would have kept my hands– and cock– away from her after she told me no. But I know it works sometimes to turn it around on her and make her feel guilty about not giving me what I want, so I give it a try now. "You are just so hot, and I love you so much, you know I didn't mean to hurt you."

"You tore my clothes off and didn't even care that I was begging you to stop. I was crying and you wouldn't listen." Her voice is cracking, I can tell reliving that night is hard for her to be doing right now. "You hurt me."

I know I should not be turned on right now, but the memory she's sharing with me to get a response of shame is actually making my cock hard.

Ripping her skirt from her body and slamming her on the bed facedown, I remember pounding her so hard my balls ached the next day. I fucked her while she lay there crying and then came on her face, mixing my come with her tears.

I had gone into the bathroom to clean up and when I came out with a wet towel for her she'd already gone. I knew she would talk to me again, even though she's a fucking prude she does want me to be happy and in her own stupid way she fucking loves me.

"I know baby," I put on my best apology voice; even to my own ears, I sound sincere. "You know I'm sorry, right? You know I didn't want to hurt you."

"Yes." That simple three- letter word means that she has forgiven me, found enough reason to blame herself and is now back in the palm of my hand.

Stupid fucking girl.

"I really need to see you, I have been missing you."

"Me too."

"But, I have to be here for a few more days, I can't miss the funeral."

"I could come." And that's the exact response I needed to hear.

"You sure you want to?"

"I think I should be there for you."

"I think so too, how bout you get your stuff packed and head over right away."

"Ok, I'll see you soon, Tyler. Thanks for the apology."

"I *am* sorry, babe. You're such a sweet girl, I'll see you soon."

I drop my phone on the bed and head downstairs, I feel a rush of excitement thinking about her being here. My throbbing cock takes me down the next flight of stairs to the basement- sex- dungeon and my pants are off before I know what I'm doing. I am so hard right now and the sight of the sheet-covered table sends my dick into an impossibly harder state.

I crave what's under that cover and it drives me crazy to be able to use it whenever I see fit. I waste no time inserting the pussy tube that had been drying since the night before and slipping my cock into the cavity, the warmth is there right away and the tight grip around my cock lessons some of the need.

I spread her legs wide, fuck it until I'm dizzy and need to come. This time I pull out and spray come all over her full tits. She'll be ready to fuck again sooner if I don't have to clean the tube- insert each time. I remember my father possibly sharing the same idea in those videos from his safe deposit box. He had pulled out, too.

Although there is really no need to worry about running out of holes, there are two others I could use as back- up. I almost have the energy to give one of those a go, as well, but I want to hold off for Cammie– pound that bitch into submission. I'm not the perfect boyfriend, but I do like to make sure she gets off when we fuck.

I figure I'll go out and see the town while I get some fucking food for this place, since my mother is most definitely *not* grocery shopping.

I chuckle to myself, she's not doing anything but being a fucking come receptacle, but that's how I always thought of her. I can think back on those days where she was warping her young son, turning him into a deviant– a degenerate, she was so hungry for me, and now she can have her fill, I'll feed her load after load of my nut.

***

The grocery store, and everything in this town leading up to it, is exactly as I remember it, the same people walking the same streets, the same houses looking exactly the same. I'm feeling a little more nostalgic than I was when first arriving. It feels comfortable, like the hometown I grew up in– familiar. I think I like it.

On the way home from the store I stop at my father's– now my car dealership. The man behind the desk is Bill; he has been here since I was a kid and loved to come hang out with my father while he worked.

He recognizes me right away. "Tyler! You're looking great, a real man you've become."

"Thank you, Bill. You're looking well; my father must have been treating you nicely."

"As always, the best man I knew." He seems to become lost in the fond memories.

"I'm just going to take a quick look around." I'm not sure why I've come, feeling more and more like I belong here, maybe?

"Will you be staying… taking over for your old man?" He seems hopeful.

Like many in this town relying on one of the few jobs with benefits, working for a man who actually gave a shit about his employees. I'm sure he must be worried about losing his job if I were to sell the place, not knowing whether the buyer would keep everyone on board or hire a new crew, or simply start over and make it something completely different. The lot is prime real- estate, overlooking the most beautiful parts of the town, right off the highway; it gets a lot of drive by traffic.

"I'm not sure enough to say quite yet." I see the hope in his eyes die a little; he knows that I ran from here long ago. Maybe he assumes I'd still be in that frame of mind. Maybe I am. I feel almost sorry enough to say yes just to ease his tension, but I can't– not until I'm sure.

I wave to the familiar people I pass, a nice smile that says I'm here on business plastered to my face.

My father's office is the same– the man absolutely loved routine. I sit behind the desk for no real reason; I only want to see what it feels like, mostly. What it would be like to step into my father's shoes and be the younger version of him in a career I only know enough about to skate by.

I know I am capable enough to learn along the way before anyone would notice I don't know a fucking thing about it. That eases my mind a little, although I'm not really so much stressed out about this leap as maybe anxiety- ridden about leaving the old life I built all by myself and trading it in for the life of my father. I don't want anyone to think I couldn't make it on my own. I could and I did it fucking well.

I shuffle the papers sprawled across his desk, not finding anything amusing enough to focus on, I stand and head back out the way I came. "See you later, Bill. Got somethings I need to sort out. You will be the first to hear my decision." I look him in the eyes and say it with feeling.

I see relief in his eyes as I speak, he knows he will have a heads up about my choice before some head honcho waltzes in and starts barking orders.

I think the whole way home about what life would be like living here. Maybe I *could* do it and even if I couldn't hack it, I know I'd be able to leave with no issue and start over. I have done it before with far less resources.

My house appears before I'm ready to be home, I sit in the driveway staring at the structure I have so many fond memories of and so many horrific things buried here that it repulses me almost equally. I'll have to reflect on those the next few days to see if the good outweighs the bad– if I'd be able to erase the negativity from this house.

Chapter Ten

The day goes by slowly; waiting for Cammie to show up is taking forever. The girl is always in her own world, on her own time. The long drive has me impatient. I can't wait too much longer to get my hands on her. I know some may think I've ruined my chances with her, but I'm a great manipulator and I'm confident in my ability to change her mind about me.

I kill time reading my father's notes again, I'm shocked that he has come up with this idea, let alone executed it perfectly. I'm proud of him for being more than just a business man, he has proven to be quite ingenious.

It makes me wonder what I'd be capable of if I wanted something bad enough– if I put my mind to something like my father had, would I be smart enough to do it? I'd like to think so.

Cammie's text comes in; telling me she's about an hour out still, her GPS is leading the way here. She's so awful at directions, barely able to distinguish her left from her right.

I decide to go to the basement, I don't know when I'll have another chance to get down there with Cammie here, and though I'm confident in my ability to fuck her the second she walks in, I know she won't let me inside her ass, which is want I want right now.

My cock is rock hard, a mind of its own driving me forward to the tight hole I'm thinking about. As I lube up my cock with the bottle my father has created to be used in conjunction with my mother's body, I'm thinking of all the times she had me do this to her while she was alive.

I slide into her back hole effortlessly, not having to worry about the pain it would be causing. I thrust deep inside, forcing my way into the deepest parts of her ass. It feels like I remember it feeling, tight and warm, the friction building my release, my balls tighten and I let myself fill the cavity with the pent up nut they have been carrying around.

Fuck... I will never get enough of this thing. Best fucking invention ever. The feel of a real woman– her being one and all, coupled with the fact that she is silent and won't deny me anything I'd think to do to her.

I tuck her back under the sheet, flattening her limbs I pat her on her thigh, telling her 'thank you for being such a good sport', and am still chuckling as I lock up the basement again.

I'm hardly done with the task when the doorbell rings. I must have been down there longer than I thought. I really get lost in that thing.

"Tyler! I'm so sorry I wasn't here for you when I first heard the news about your dad, I feel awful that you have been dealing with this alone." She kisses me hard and I let her.

"It's ok babe, you're here now." I squeeze her ass as she presses herself against me. If I hadn't just come I would bend her the fuck over the couch and take her pussy hard, but I did, so it will have to wait.

She's grinding herself against me like she wants me to.

Fucking idiot.

Girls like her are so predictable, it almost makes me want to send her right out the door again, turn her around and get her the fuck out of here.

I'd have more fun with Jamie than her, she likes the way I fuck her and she's not complicated. I huff and pull her up the stairs to my room; taking her bags with us, I set them on top of the comforter and leave her quickly to unpack so she doesn't think I've brought her upstairs to fuck her.

I know she should be hungry and I take the fresh groceries from around the kitchen and prepare a meal I'm sure she'll be likely to finish– macaroni and cheese, it is practically the only thing she likes.

I put a ground up pill in hers, step one in my father's process, I have to empty her and the laxative should do the trick. I made the decision the second I saw her; I don't want her like this anymore.

She comes down just as I'm finishing up, I hand her a bowl and make one for myself. We eat in relative silence, my excitement keeping my thoughts elsewhere. I watch captivated as she takes bite after bite of her contaminated food.

We start a television show and shortly after, she excuses herself, saying only that she has a stomachache.

My cock throbs, waiting for her to be done; I can hardly keep my hands off it. Luckily, she comes back down awhile later interrupting my internal debate. She says she is too wiped- out to finish the program and wants to go to bed. I follow her up and lie next to her sleeping body, finally falling asleep myself hours later with the thoughts of what is to come in the morning swirling around my sleepy head.

The morning comes quickly, I'm not very rested, Cammie spent most of the night in the bathroom. Step one should be done now, she couldn't have had too much to get rid of– her small appetite can't have her full of too much.

She rolls over and wraps her arms around me, I follow suit and hug her for a few moments before saying we should get up. She seems disappointed but comes downstairs with me.

I hand her a bottle of water and brew myself a single cup of coffee. I watch as she drinks until it's gone. I don't want her having too much more than that. I just need to make sure she is flushed out and then we can begin the next step, the one I'm more excited about than I thought I'd be.

I didn't know that this would be so much fun… the plotting and manipulating. She has no idea what's in her future, and I can't wait to see her in mine– lain out and spread wide– ready to take me. First step will be fucking her virgin asshole– primed and ready for me like my father did to his homemade sex doll.

I ask her how she feels this morning.

"I'm ok, I feel much better than last night... must have been all the stress I felt over leaving you alone over here."

"Well, you can make it up to me right now– if you want," I say in the tone I'm sure she knows by now as the flirty- guy- who- wants- to- fuck.

"Ok." She licks her lips and I know she gets the message.

"Come on." I grab her hand and lead her to the couch; I really meant it when I said I wanted to fuck her bent over it. "Take your clothes off. Let me see you."

She does as she was told.

Fuck she has such a tight little body, high, perky tits with nipples that make my mouth water. The gap between her thighs coupled with her meaty pussy makes it easy to see the lips from where I sit in front of her.

I pull her over to me and spread her thighs wider, one on either side of my own naked thighs; I sit her down on top of me, pushing my fingers deep inside of her. I plunge my fingers into her like that until she's clawing at me, the wet sounds of her pussy filling the room.

I pick her up by her armpits and push her down onto the couch, shoving her face into the cushion. She goes to make a noise of argument but bites her tongue, knowing she shouldn't voice it right now, not with her feeling so bad about my dear 'ol daddy passing and her leaving me to fend for myself.

I take advantage of that, going a little rougher than I know I'm allowed. Even after her having a valid excuse to push me away– *fuck*, I practically *raped* her last time we fucked. But she stays where I put her, spreading her thighs wide enough to accommodate me. Her pink little asshole calling to me– *that* I'll wait for though, I have proof that it will be better when we're done here.

I slip right into her wet hole, all the way in, my balls pressing right against her soft mound. I don't fuck her yet though, instead I reach around to the front of her and work her clit like I know will have her lost in an orgasm in no time.

She moans and fucks herself on my cock, I don't help her, I just hold my pole in place for her pleasure. And, just like I knew would happen, her pussy tightens and convulses around my cock. That's when I finally fuck her, I go hard and fast, pounding her until she can hardly hold herself up. I am shoving her body hard into the back of the couch, grunting hard– almost missing my moment and coming but I'm able to pull back in time to hold off my nut.

I reach for my 2- inch chisel I had tucked into the cushion and align it with the base of her neck. She's so lost in what I'm doing to her pussy that she has no idea what is happening right behind her back.

Finding the exact area indicated by my father, I draw my arm back and thrust it hard into the spot, I feel right away that it has worked, her body goes limp, I keep fucking her until I'm done– which is only seconds later, the feel of her lifeless body under me practically forces the come from my balls.

I recover quickly and drag her tiny body to the basement where I'm told to hang her upside down by her ankles. I feel for the spot on the neck to sever her jugular vein, which should pull the blood from her body. My father has the perfect set up– a drain in the floor under the ankle holster makes for easy clean up.

That should take a while I'm told, so I go upstairs to shower the smears of blood covering my naked body.

I can hardly wait to get back to the basement. I rush my shower and am back in no time, just a pair of boxers on.

Epilogue

The next few days I followed my father's instructions to the letter, going between creating my very own fuck doll and making time with my father's creation. I feel like I've never felt before, I'm exhilarated. I fucking love this, the two most perfect fucking specimens– mine to fuck when and how I want. There is no other way to explain it but to say I am content. That's what I am right now, perfectly content.

My father's funeral went off without a hitch and I'm back in the basement now, finishing everything up with my little 'Cammie' doll, inserting her very own fuck tubes and sponging both bodies off for the day. She looks as good as my 'mother' doll.

Not too bad for my first try.

I told Bill at the shop that I'd be staying on and keeping everything as my father had set about doing. I gave him a promotion to general manager, knowing his knowledge will come in handy along the way.

I redid the house, redecorating it to fit my style, gutting most of it to accommodate me. I absolutely love it here now; the town feels like home.

They think my mother ran off with a new man, something my father had been telling them for a while now. It was an easy lie, the town knew my mother couldn't keep her hands to herself, she fucked many of the men in town while still alive and 'happy' with my father. While keeping our activities a secret she still had a need for more.

Fucking whore.

There is a new woman in town, she caught my eye the first time I saw her in the shop, she came in looking to trade in her old car, fresh start and all, she had to upgrade her wheels. I think I'll grab her and add her to my collection.

My father may have been happy with just my mother, but I have a need for variety that hasn't been quenched yet. Our first date is tonight. I guess we'll see how it goes.

The End

Remember to leave a review
I appreciate the time you've spent reading and

I would love to know what you thought about it.

Thank you!

Printed in Great Britain
by Amazon